The Christmas Sten...

978-1-72-933341-9

Follow M.S.French on most, popular social media
to hear about new books and projects:
@MSFrenchBooks

The Christmas Stench

Written & Illustrated By
M.S. French

On a fine winters day,
Playing *games* on the go,
Good friends run around,
Making **prints** in the snow...

At the *end* of the game,

Little Leo had won.

It was *time* to go home,

Before daylight was gone.

Then young Leo remembered
That Christmas was nigh.
So he turned to his friends
And he waved them goodbye.

As he started to walk

With his head in a dream,

All that Leo could think of,

Was custard and cream...

There were *gifts* on his mind
That he could not forget.
A cute cat, or a dog,
Or a cow for a pet!

Maybe cars, or toy trains
To be raced on the floor.
Or a gun or a sword,
Or a tank to play war!

But when Leo got out
Of that dream, he could see.
That the sun would soon set.
It's already past three!

He *had* to get home
For the Christmas Eve meal.
Eat up, or no presents.
Yes, **that** was the deal.

So he hurried back home,

Like an *elf* in a rush.

Right through town

Where the snow,

Had all melted to slush.

Looking nowhere but up,

Lights were hard to ignore.

Leo **ran** past the lot,

Aiming straight for his door.

Coming into the hall,

There was no one about.

Had they started to eat?

Did they move on without?

Now before he could know,

Something nasty arose.

Eyes *can't* see it well.

Maybe try with your nose...

Little Leo then sniffed...

"What on earth is that **SMELL**?

And where did it come from?"

Leo *couldn't* quite tell.

He decided at once,

That he had to find out.

Little Leo was set,

To *search* and to scout!

So the kitchen was first,

Maybe milk had gone bad.

And someone was there,

Which made Leo quite glad...

It was Mother and Gran,

Still preparing the food!

They both *LOVE* to cook big.

It's that Christmas Eve mood.

But the stench wasn't there.

Well, it wasn't the same.

Little Leo believed

Someone else was to blame!

Leo snuck down the hall,
First his sister he found.
On the carpet alone,
She had fun with a sound.

All the food she just ate,

Came back up pretty quick.

With her hand, a big **SPLASH**!

Baby *Gem* played with *sick*.

But the stench was still strong.

Was it going to spread?

If it got any worse,

It could grow its own *head!*

Little Leo went on
To hear Father and Fin.
They were boxing all day,
Throwing punches to win.

Leo kept out the way,
For his nose to forget.
He had tried to look in
And that room
stank of *SWEAT!*

But the stench was still strong.

A big funk in the air.

If it got any worse,

We'd see *arms* and spiked *hair!*

"Maybe Rina's to blame!"
Leo thought as he ran.
"I will catch that mean stench!"
At least, that was his plan.

He was right, but not quite.
Leo saw with a glance.
In a *cloud* of *perfume*,
She would spray to a dance.

But the stench was still strong,
Although less of a fright.
If it got any worse,
It might *kick*, it might *bite!*

So then what could it be,

If not Polly and Lane?

Two friends having tea

In a **BOAT**. Not a plane!

There was not much to smell

But the scent of mint green.

They were dressed in nice clothes

And the bedroom was clean.

And then mother called out.
"Dinner's done, come on down!
This *food* will go quick
And the *fish* wears a crown!"

Just as Leo ran down

To be first to a seat;

He heard *hums* from the hall,

So just who would he meet?

It was *Grampa*, you see,

But behind the white door.

In the toilet he'd *sing*

And at times, even snore!

WC

Little Leo was certain,

The stench came from here.

I might also add happy,

That his conscience felt clear.

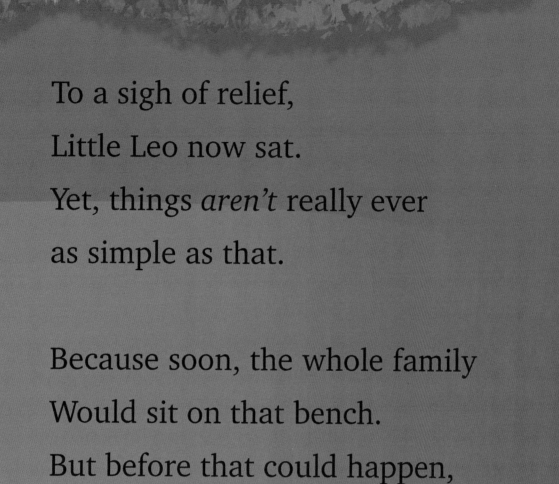

To a sigh of relief,
Little Leo now sat.
Yet, things *aren't* really ever
as simple as that.

Because soon, the whole family
Would sit on that bench.
But before that could happen,
They might smell that mean stench.

Sure enough, they all did.
But it's pretty clear why.
It was there, in plain sight
And I'd not call it shy.

They shut mouths, covered eyes
And *ALL* pinched their noses.
The Christmas Eve stench,
Did *NOT* smell like roses!

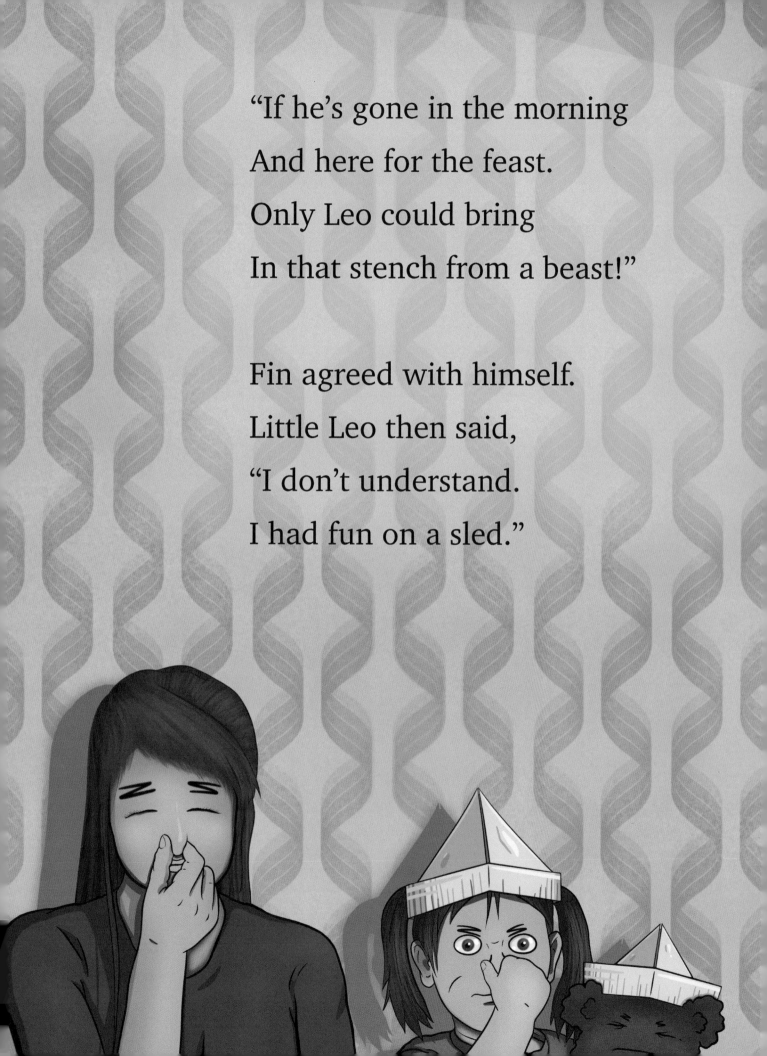

"If he's gone in the morning
And here for the feast.
Only Leo could bring
In that stench from a beast!"

Fin agreed with himself.
Little Leo then said,
"I don't understand.
I had fun on a sled."

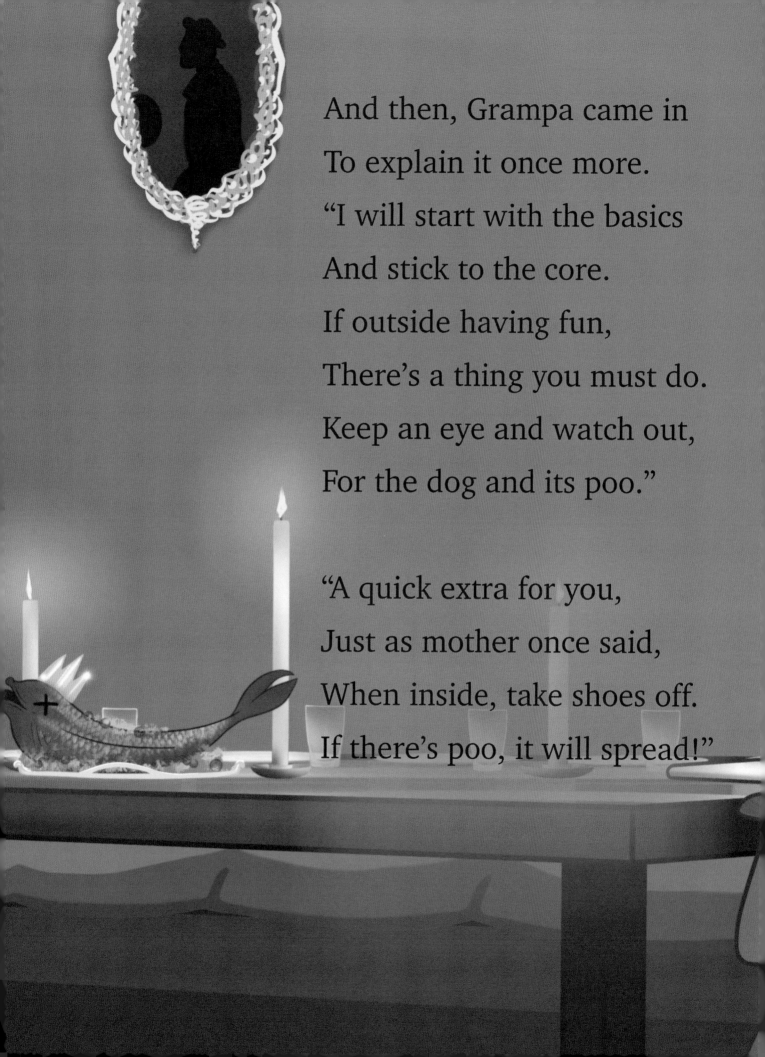

And then, Grampa came in
To explain it once more.
"I will start with the basics
And stick to the core.

If outside having fun,
There's a thing you must do.
Keep an eye and watch out,
For the dog and its poo."

"A quick extra for you,
Just as mother once said,
When inside, take shoes off.
If there's poo, it will spread!"

Little Leo went *red*,
And was scared to admit.
That his shoes were still on,
And both covered in... ***DOG POO!***

Keep an *eye* and watch *out*.
You can step in a lot.
By this time tomorrow,
You might have forgot.

There's a place you should look
When a stench visits you;
It's not other people,
But the *sole* of your *shoe*.

The End

Printed in Great Britain
by Amazon